{geography focus}

MOVING PEOPLE
{Migration and Settlement}

Louise Spilsbury

Raintree
Chicago, Illinois

Cover, text design, and graphs by Marta White
Map diagrams by Guy Holt
Technical diagrams by Nives Porcellato and Andy Craig

Printed in China

10 09 08 07 06
10 9 8 7 6 5 4 3 2 1

Library of Congress Cataloging-in-Publication Data
Spilsbury, Louise.
  Moving people : migration and settlement / Louise Spilsbury.
    p. cm. -- (Geography focus)
  Includes bibliographical references and index.
  ISBN-13: 978-1-4109-1115-5 (library binding-hardcover)
  ISBN-10: 1-4109-1115-2 (library binding-hardcover)
  1. Human settlements--Juvenile literature. 2. Cities and towns--Growth--Juvenile literature. 3. Migration, Internal--Juvenile literature. 4. Forced migration--Juvenile literature. I. Title.
  HT65.S67 2006
  307--dc22
                                        2005028658

Acknowledgments
The author and publisher are grateful to the following for permission to reproduce copyright material: AAP/AFP Photo/Choo Youn-Kong: p. **26**; APL/Corbis/Yann Arthus-Bertrand p. **35**, /Michael Brennan: p. **33**, /Howard Davies: p. **22**, /Jay Dickman: p. **13** (lower), /ER Productions: p. **28**, /Viviane Moos: p. **24**, /Peter Turnley p. **38**; /Robert van der Hilst: p. **36**, /Wild Country: p. **8**; Barry S. Doe, FCLIT, C.MATH, MIMA: p. **34**; Ecoscene/Sue Anderson: p. **42**; Denise B. Fong: p. **41**; Getty Images/Hulton Archive/Wood: p. **14**, /Tony Stone: pp. **18, 32**; Liaison/Scott Peterson: p. **25**; Lonely Planet Images/Chris Mellor: p. **30**, /Ariadne Van Zandbergen: p. **13** (middle left), /Julia Wilkinson: p. **11**; NASA/Goddard Space Flight Center/Craig Mayhew and Robert Simmon: p. **39**; Photo Edit Inc./David Young-Wolff: p. **43**; Photolibrary.com: p. **10**, /Index Stock: pp. **4, 9**, /OSF: p. **6**, /Photo Researchers: p. **15**; Reuters/PictureMedia/Jayanta Shaw: p. **20**; Still Pictures/Mark Edwards: p. **16**. All other images PhotoDisc.

Cover photograph of city reproduced with permission of PhotoDisc; inset image of Rwandan refugees arriving at Benaco camp, Tanzania, reproduced with permission of APL/Corbis/Howard Davies.

{Contents}

Words that are printed in bold, **like this**,
are explained in the Glossary on page 46.

{Where People Live}

It might be hard for most of us to imagine, but the first people on Earth did not have a place to call home. They followed herds of animals that they hunted for meat and fur. They ate fruits and leaves that they gathered along the way. They lived in temporary shelters such as caves and never stayed in one place for long.

The first settlements

About 10,000 years ago, there was a huge change. People became farmers. They began to grow their own plants and to keep their own animals. Because they could provide the food they needed in one place, they started to settle down. These first settlements usually had a small group of buildings around the farmland.

The world's oldest city

In 2000 **archaeologists** uncovered remains of what they believe is the world's oldest known city. Hamoukar in Syria was home to 25,000 people about 6,000 years ago.

*Some people still live a **nomadic** life. These people travel around Iran and live in temporary shelters.*

The growth of settlements

By farming, people could increase the amount of food they produced. This meant that more people could live off one area of land, and the **population** began to grow. Over the years, as settlements got bigger, there were different kinds of jobs to do. For example, people worked in hospitals, schools, and shops. Gradually, towns and cities developed. Today, most people live in permanent settlements like these.

Around the world

This map of the world shows **population density**. That means it shows an average number of people per square mile living in different parts of the world. The more darkly an area is shaded on the map, the greater its density. That does not mean that more people live there. For example, China is the country with the largest number of people in the world. However, the population density over most of China is lower than a country like the United Kingdom. The UK has far fewer people, but they all live close to one another on a small island. China is a huge country, so people are spread out more. Some areas, such as Greenland, have both a very low population and a low population density because the weather is too extreme for many people to live there.

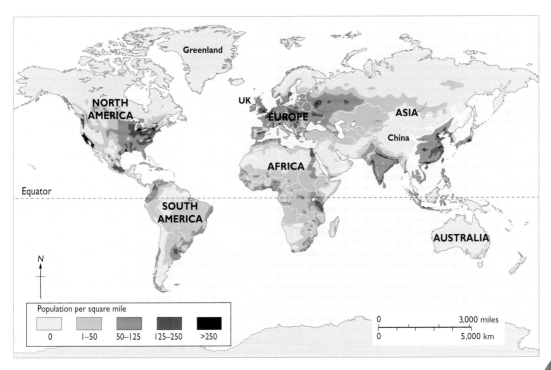

This map shows where most people in the world live.

{Living on the Land}

The **site** of a settlement is where the settlement is built. Two important factors that influence people when they choose a site for a settlement are **terrain** and **climate**. The terrain is the shape, features, and type of land in an area. The climate is the kind of weather you usually get in an area.

Mountains and deserts

Some people live in mountain areas, but more people live in the flat areas of land below mountains. The steep, rocky slopes of a mountain are hard to build on or farm. Moreover, mountain settlements can be very cold and isolated. It takes a long time to travel to cities below to get goods or to use services like hospitals. Deserts may be flatter, but they are too hot and dry for many settlements. Modern technologies such as air conditioning have made desert living more comfortable, however. Improved water transportation has also helped people to farm in desert areas.

People who live in isolated mountain regions like this one in Nepal have to produce almost everything they need for themselves.

In the past

Today, we can transport fuel and other **resources** that people need over long distances. However, in the past, people only had carts and animals to travel on or to carry things. There were no underground pipes to transport water. They had to build settlements near the resources that they needed, such as rivers, **fertile** land that was good for farming, or forests for wood.

Many settlements were built on hills because that made them easy to defend. That is why you usually see castles on hills. People would build their villages on the hillside near the castle and use the flat land at the bottom of the hill for farming.

Coast and country

Australia is a good example of how climate and terrain affect the site of settlements. The central area of Australia is hot and dry. A large part of it is desert. In parts the soil is too poor for farming. Most of Australia's **population** lives around the coast, where it is cooler.

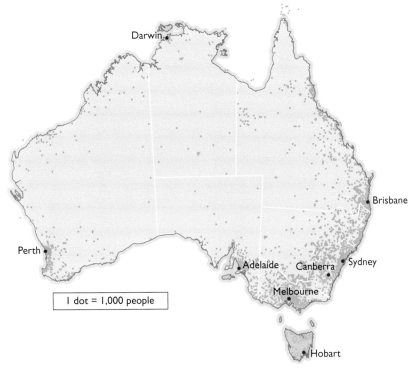

I dot = 1,000 people

This map of Australia shows the more densely populated areas on the coast and the largely uninhabited (not lived in) area in the middle of the country.

{The Development of Settlements}

Many settlements have developed, or grown, in areas that provide people with work. The **function** of a settlement is its main economic activity or purpose. For example, some settlements develop in areas where there is coal or other minerals that can be mined.

Settlement functions

Many settlements have grown up around a particular **resource** or **industry**. For example, the city of Johannesburg in South Africa developed close to rich goldfields. Some settlements developed at coastal areas with good natural harbors. Most of the people who lived there were connected with the fishing industry. As these places grew, they became important **ports**. Ports are settlements where goods can be brought in and out of a country by ship. Many of today's big cities, such as Boston and London, became important as major ports.

All the major settlements of Egypt are along the banks of the mighty Nile River. Boats can travel almost all the way along it, carrying goods to and from towns along the way.

Sites of religious importance

Some settlements develop in places that are important to particular religions. The city of Varanasi in India grew at an important place on the Hindu holy Ganges River. Makkah in Saudi Arabia is a holy city for Muslims because it was the home of Mohammad, who started their religion.

Changing settlements

Settlements are always changing. They may get bigger or change their function. Silicon Valley, California, was once a quiet, fruit-growing area. Since the 1950s, it has become an important center for new computer technologies. This has meant a huge increase in the size and number of towns there for the people involved in these industries.

Some settlements get smaller or disappear. The city of Fatepur Sikri in India, built in 1571, was supposed to be an important city. However, the leader who built the city left because it didn't have a good water supply. The city gradually declined, and today it is in ruins.

The town of Nantucket, Massachusetts, was once a center for whaling. Today, most people work in hotels, restaurants, or other businesses catering to tourists.

{ Kinds of Settlements }

If you took a helicopter trip around the world, you would see many different kinds of settlements below. The way a settlement's streets are laid out, the way the land is used, and the particular styles of its buildings say a lot about where it is, when it developed, and its **function**.

Grids and circles

Many towns and cities are laid out in a grid pattern. The streets run in a set of lines running from side to side and up and down. Many cities in the United States, such as New York and Chicago, were planned in this way. Other cities are planned so that the streets spread out from a central point in a series of circles. Towns and cities like this have lots of houses and other buildings grouped closely together around a central point, or nucleus. They are called nucleated settlements.

Many cities have this kind of grid layout.

Spreading out

Many cities that began as smaller towns or villages long ago have grown in a more haphazard way. As the **population** grew, new buildings spread out from the center of the settlement without a fixed plan. Some settlements that developed along trade routes spread along a road or a river. This kind of settlement is called a linear settlement. That means it is a settlement that developed in a line.

Shared cultures

Towns and cities that have a similar culture or religion often follow the same pattern. Many Muslim cities have similar layouts. At the middle of the cities of Cairo and Damascus are the main mosque (the Muslim place of worship,) the main marketplace, and a palace. These places were the focus of people's lives, so the cities spread out from them.

Many people live in traditional villages near farms. This settlement is in a valley in Bhutan, in south-central Asia. The main buildings are on a hill, with farms on the terraced (stepped) hillsides and in the valley below.

{Buildings Around the World}

All over the world, people are doing similar kinds of things in the houses and other buildings they use. Homes are somewhere to study, sleep, and relax and to prepare and eat our meals. If houses and homes around the world are used in similar ways, why do they often look so very different?

Building materials

Today, many people can afford to **import** materials they want to use for their houses, such as special stone from another country. But in poorer countries, buildings are often made using materials that can be found or bought locally. For example, in desert areas where trees are rare, many people live in mud huts or houses constructed from sun-dried clay bricks. Older houses built near forests may be almost completely made from wood.

Climate and homes

In some parts of the world, the design of buildings is determined by the weather. For example, in some very hot countries, houses have walls made of a kind of straw matting. Like blinds on a window, these walls can be rolled up to let in breezes or rolled down to keep out sunlight. In very cold countries, the windows are often small, and the walls are thick to keep the warmth in.

Style and design

The style and design of buildings often differs across countries because of their different religions. For example, many Hindu temples in India are tall and narrower at the top, so that their shape looks like the Himalayan mountains to the north of India. Muslim temples in the Middle East and around the world are called mosques. They usually have a dome (rounded) roof. Christian churches are often built in the shape of a cross and have a tower with a tall steeple.

Here are different houses around the world: (clockwise from top) a two-story timber house with a porch to protect against the Sun in the United States; a sturdy concrete apartment block in Russia that can house many; a house on stilts on a river in Peru; and grass huts in Kenya.

{Case Study} Hong Kong

When you look at the two photos on these pages, it's hard to believe that the Hong Kong of 2000 (below right) could be the same place as shown in the picture from 1900 (below). Hong Kong is a settlement that drastically grew and changed over the course of the 20th century.

Past and present

In 1900 there were about 100,000 people living in the **port** of Hong Kong. Hong Kong is located on the southeast coast of China, but at that time the British government ran China. Although China has been independent since 1949, Great Britain ruled Hong Kong until 1997. In the 20th century, during times of unrest in China, many people moved from China to Hong Kong. The population grew rapidly, and by 1950 it had reached two million. The increased number of people began cheaply producing goods, such as textiles, plastics, toys, radios, and watches, that were sold all over the world. Today, there are almost seven million people living in Hong Kong.

As a fishing port at the beginning of the 20th century, Hong Kong housed only 100,000 people.

Perfect port

Hong Kong itself has no **natural resources**, such as oil, to sell. However, it is the biggest and deepest port in the world and is one of the busiest shipping centers in the world. More than 30,000 vessels visit the port every year. Ships load up with millions of goods from the rest of China, taking them to be sold to the rest of the world.

Going up

The growth in the number of people and in the amount of wealth in Hong Kong between 1900 and 2000 made a huge difference to the settlements there. By the early 1970s, businesses needed many new buildings to work in and people needed new homes to live in. The problem with Hong Kong is that mountains surround it and there is a limited amount of flat land to build on. The only way to go was up. Today, Hong Kong's skyline is full of high-rise buildings, and it has several of the tallest buildings in the whole of Asia.

*Hong Kong was once the quiet home of fishermen and farmers. Today, it is a huge and thriving city with the highest **population density** in the world. There are roughly 2,450 people per square mile.*

{People on the Move}

Today, most people live in a settlement of some kind, but they don't necessarily stay in the same settlement in the same country for their whole lives. When people move from one place to another, this is called migration. People may **migrate** permanently or for a limited time. They may move to a new place in the same country or to a new country altogether.

Why do people migrate?

People move to new places for a variety of reasons. Many people migrate because they have no choice. They move because they have to. It may not be safe to live in their home anymore, perhaps because of war or the risk of a **natural disaster** such as flooding. Some people have to migrate to find work.

302

Z   419

LH 1122

LH 1906

*These migrants have packed all their belongings into a truck to move from **rural** Mexico to Mexico City.*

Many people migrate somewhere new simply because they prefer it there. They may move to a place with a warmer or cooler **climate** or to somewhere that they think has more attractive surroundings. When people migrate, they may often choose to go somewhere because they have friends or family there. For example, many people who migrate from Poland move to Chicago, because there is already a large **population** of Polish people living there.

Migration routes

International migration is when people move from one country to another. This map shows the main international migration patterns at the end of the 20th century. The largest numbers of people on the move **emigrated** from Latin America and Asia to North America, or they emigrated from Eastern Europe and North Africa into Northern and Western Europe. Millions of people from Africa and Asia also moved to the Middle East. In all these cases, people were moving from poorer countries to wealthier countries with more job opportunities.

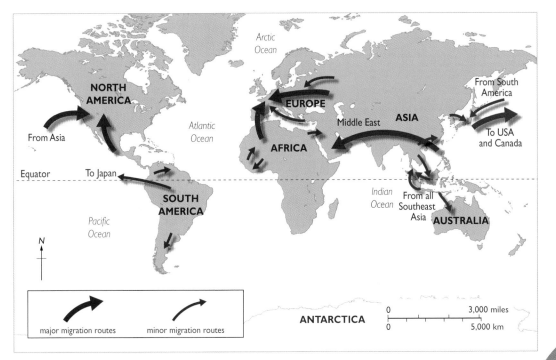

This map shows the major patterns of international migration in the early 1990s.

{Case Study} The United States

The original inhabitants of the United States were Native Americans. Today, Native Americans form only a tiny proportion of the total **population** of the United States. Most Americans today **migrated** from other countries or have grandparents or great-grandparents who were **immigrants**.

American people

The first settlers arrived in the U.S. by boat from Europe in the 1600s. Some of these people left their home country to find a place to live where they could follow their religion freely. Gradually, more and more Europeans came, and from 1800 the population grew rapidly.

A multicultural society

In the biggest cities in the United States today, there are people of a variety of different nationalities with different cultures and languages. In Los Angeles, over a quarter of the population speaks Spanish.

When people move to a new country, they often choose to live near friends or family who originally came from the same country. This is Chinatown in New York, an area of the city where the majority of people originated from China.

Some people came to the United States to escape trouble in their own country. For example, many people came from Ireland in the mid-19th century to escape a **famine**, during which many people starved to death. Other people were forced to come. For example, many Africans were brought to the United States to work as slaves on large farms called plantations. Others came for the chance to buy land and start farms in the large areas of open country. For them, the United States was the "land of opportunity."

Number crunching

This bar chart shows the numbers of immigrants who entered the United States between 1900 and 1998. It also shows the countries from which they came.

From 1900 to 1930, most immigrants were from Europe. Between 1940 and 1950, immigration suddenly decreased because of World War II. After the 1960s, the number of immigrants increased again as people came to the U.S. hoping to make a better life for themselves. In the last 25 years, most of the people who migrated to the U.S. have come from Asia or Latin America.

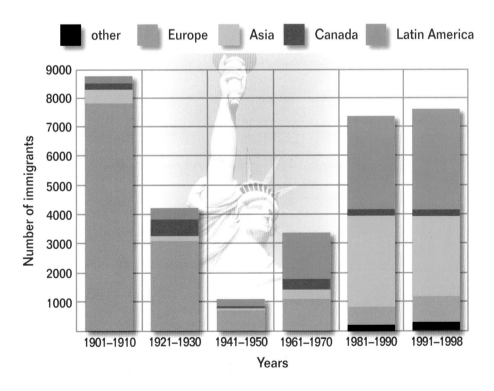

This bar chart shows the number and origins of immigrants to the United States during different periods in the 1900s.

{Traveling to Work}

All around the world, people travel to work. For many people, this means a daily commute. They travel to their workplace and back home again on the same day. For millions of others, even finding work means **migrating** to find a job in a new town, city, or even country.

Temporary travel

Some people migrate for seasonal work. They may travel to a fruit-farming area within their own country to pick apples or strawberries for a season. Other people travel abroad for long periods of time for work. They may do this to earn more or because they cannot find work in their own country. For example, young men from Mexico travel to the United States to work on farms, and young women from the Philippines travel to other countries nearby to find work as servants in people's homes. These people are called **migrant workers**. Over 35 million people work in other countries like this.

Millions of commuters around the world rely on public transportation to take them to work and back home each day. This is a packed train in India.

Push and pull factors

Push and pull factors make people migrate. Push factors are reasons people want to leave a place, such as lack of work. Pull factors are reasons people want to move somewhere new, such as better-paying jobs.

Permanent positions

Some people move permanently to a new place to get a more interesting or better-paying job. Many other people migrate because they have to—for example, if they cannot find work where they live. Millions of people move from the country to a city to find work because they can no longer make a living farming the land. This is called **rural** to **urban** migration.

Moving on

This line graph shows the huge rural to urban migration in Mexico between 1900 and 1990. One reason for this change was that companies from countries such as the United States opened up factories there. These factories paid low wages, but the wages were higher than people could earn as farmers. So, many workers migrated to the cities.

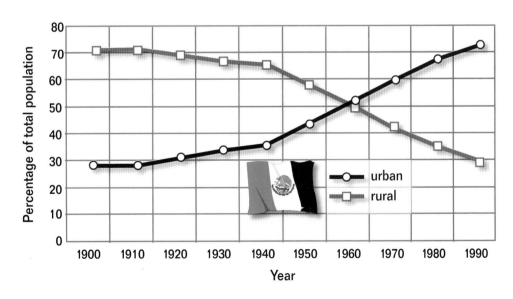

This line graph shows Mexico's urban and rural population from 1900 to 1990.

{Escaping Conflict}

Imagine being forced to leave your home, perhaps in the middle of a cold night. You don't have time to pack a bag or enough space to carry all your favorite things. You have to walk many miles to escape danger. This is what really happens to many **refugees** around the world.

A refugee is someone who has been forced to flee his or her home to escape danger and is afraid to return there. Many people become refugees to escape war and conflict. Refugees may **migrate** to safer parts of their own country or go to other countries. Today, there are about 37 million people in the world who have been forced to leave their own settlements and seek shelter elsewhere. After a while, it may be safe for refugees to return home, perhaps once a war is over. But some may choose to stay in the new place or country permanently.

These refugees have left their homes in Rwanda, Africa, where hundreds of thousands of Tutsi people were murdered by Hutu soldiers. They are traveling to a camp in Tanzania.

Refugee ratings

This bar chart shows the countries from which the largest numbers of refugees were forced to flee their homes in the 1990s.

The worst case is Rwanda in Africa. There was a **civil war** there in the 1990s between the Tutsi people and the Hutu people. Hundreds of thousands of people were killed and millions escaped to countries nearby. The war ended in 1994, and since then many Rwandans have been migrating back to their homes.

The second largest number of refugees listed here came from Iraq in 1991. These refugees were Kurdish people who were made homeless as a result of attacks by Iraqi soldiers under orders from their leader, Saddam Hussein.

In 1991 more than one million refugees left the country of Somalia, on the east coast of Africa. They fled from the heavy fighting that went on between government soldiers and rebels during the civil war there.

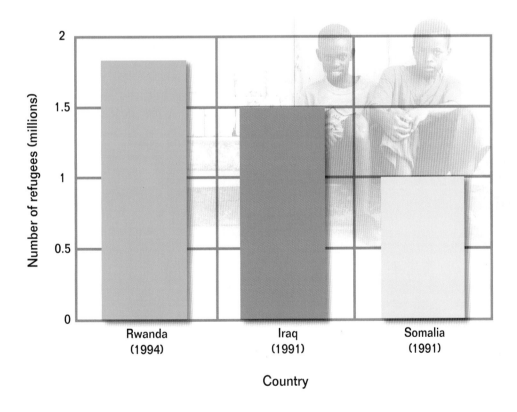

This bar chart shows the countries with the largest numbers of refugees in the 1990s.

{Case Study}
Darfur Refugees

By 2004, after two years of violence and fighting between the government and rebel groups, many people had fled their homes in Darfur, Sudan, in Africa. Over one million **refugees** escaped to other places within Darfur, and hundreds of thousands more escaped to the nearby country of Chad. Most of these people ended up in refugee camps. Refugee camps are temporary settlements of tents and shelters.

First camps

When refugees first arrive in a place, they are tired, hungry, and thirsty. They make shelters out of plastic sheets, cardboard, or whatever they can find. Darfur is a dry, desert region with only scattered trees, so it is hard to find water for drinking, cooking, and washing. At home, many of the refugees had land where they grew their own food, but most did not have enough cash to buy food from stores.

In refugee camps, people get schools running as soon as they can. It's important that children don't fall behind on their education. This might spoil their chances of getting jobs in the future.

Aid agencies

In a case like Darfur, when many poor people are forced to find a new place to live, aid agencies soon step in to help. Aid agencies are organizations such as the Red Cross or Save the Children that raise money to help people in emergencies. They provide people in a refugee camp with tents, medical help, food, water, and blankets. They try to make space for children to play and help people to set up a place to worship. They also help people find members of their families, if they have been separated. When it is safe, aid agencies try to help families get back to their homelands and rebuild their lives.

FACT!

Around the world, about 3,000 people become refugees every day. More than half of these refugees are children.

SUDAN

Large refugee camps look like a city of tents. People may stay in refugee camps like this for months or even years.

{Escaping Natural Disasters}

Floods, earthquakes, hurricanes, and **tsunamis** are **natural disasters** that can destroy whole settlements in a matter of moments. Some disasters happen without warning, but in many cases there are systems in place that can warn people in time for them to get to safety.

Before and after

The problem is that natural disasters affect people and settlements in **less-developed countries** far worse than in others. Such countries often cannot afford warning systems to help people escape, plus poor people often live in unsafe places. In Bangladesh, floods kill many poor people because they cannot afford to live in well-built houses on high, flat, safe land like rich people. They live in flimsy homes near rivers or coasts that flood. Even in **more-developed countries** such as the United States, the poor can be the greatest victims of natural disasters. The response to help victims of Hurricane Katrina in New Orleans in August 2005 was criticized because many of the city's poor, sick, and elderly citizens were left stranded by the floods.

In December 2004 a tsunami hit coastal areas in thirteen countries in the Indian Ocean, including Indonesia, Thailand, and Sri Lanka. This giant, destructive wave caused terrible damage and killed over 200,000 people.

Earthquake!

An earthquake is when the surface of Earth suddenly shakes and cracks open in places. On August 17, 1999, an earthquake near the city of Izmit, Turkey, killed more than 17,000 people. More than 66,440 houses were destroyed and 150,000 were damaged. On October 17, 1989, a similar strength earthquake rocked San Francisco and other cities in California. There, about 60 people were killed. Over 1,300 homes and businesses were destroyed and about 27,000 were damaged.

The main cause of the difference between the damage caused by these two quakes is in the kinds of settlements. The city of Izmit has many poor people living in cheaply built apartment buildings that are four to eight stories high. These buildings collapsed easily and killed people inside them. In California, lots of money, effort, and time have been dedicated to designing and making buildings that are strong enough to withstand earthquakes. The safer buildings meant that there was much less damage than there could have been.

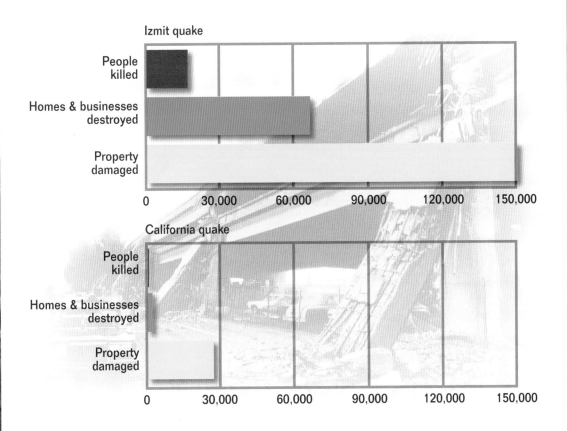

This bar chart shows the differences in death and destruction between the California and Izmit earthquakes.

{A Crowded Planet}

There are more people on Earth now than ever before. Each day, the **population** of the world increases by 200,000 people and our planet gets more crowded. Today, the world population is over six billion.

Growth rates

For most of the time that humans have been living on the planet, the population grew very slowly. Although many babies were born, most people did not reach old age because they died from disease or lack of food. Then, in the 1800s, huge improvements in medicine and **sanitation** meant that people started to live for longer. For example, babies were given **vaccinations** that protected them from illnesses that had once killed many.

In the 20th century, there was another change. Industrialization brought new farm machines and factories that could produce more food and feed the growing population. New **industries** also brought jobs and wealth so that people could afford to feed more children and improve their **standard of living**.

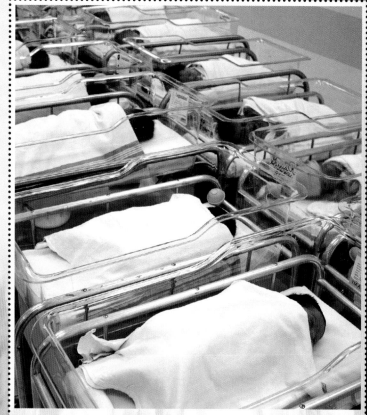

Populations grow when the birth rate is higher than the death rate. As more people live longer, the number of children being born is higher than the number of people who die.

Explaining the growth

This graph shows how the population of the world has grown since 1750. It also shows the increase in population that scientists expect to see by 2050. Some scientists believe that by 2100, numbers will level out, but this is hard to predict.

The graph shows that there are differences between population growth in **less-developed countries** compared to **more-developed countries**. In more-developed countries, such as the United States, families usually have one or two children. At this rate, the population stays steady or grows only very slowly.

In many less-developed countries, for example countries in Africa, the average number of children in a family is five. In these countries, the populations are still increasing rapidly. In some less-developed countries, such as China, families are having fewer children on average. But the population is still increasing because there are so many more young people than older people. As these young people reach adulthood, they are having children, and so the population is still increasing.

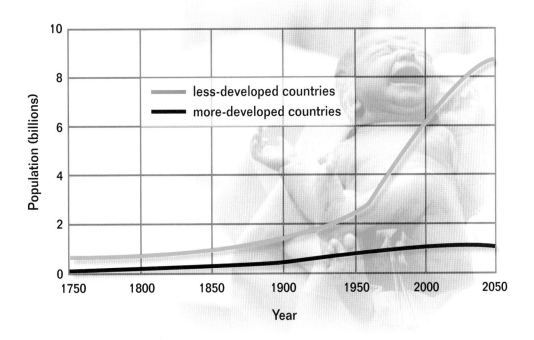

This line graph shows the world population growth from 1750 to 2050.

{Growing Cities}

As the world's **population** increases, more people live in cities than ever before. By 1900 more than one-tenth of the world's people lived in cities. Today, almost half of the people in the world already live in cities, and soon two out of three people will be city dwellers. Existing cities are getting bigger, and more new cities and towns are growing.

Why are cities growing?

A huge increase in city populations has happened in the past few decades. One of the main reasons for this is **rural** to **urban migration**. This means the number of people moving from the country into cities. When the increased number of people in a city have children, the population gets even bigger. Many people come to cities for work or because cities usually have bigger and better **services**, such as hospitals and colleges. People also like to move to cities because they have lots of leisure facilities, such as theaters, sports stadiums, and zoos.

*Tokyo, Japan, is a huge **metropolis** that is home to twelve million people.*

Changing cities

The map shows the percentage of people who live in towns and cities across the world. The darker the color, the higher the urban population. For example, a country like the U.S. has many more people living in cities (over 75 percent) than China, at 29 percent.

However, we also need to look at the chart to see how this map is likely to change. The chart shows that cities like New York grew rapidly up until 1970, but since then they have grown much more slowly or even reduced in growth. That is because some people have chosen to move out of cities into smaller towns or into the country. Cities in many of the **less-developed countries**, such as Mumbai, India, and Lagos, Nigeria, are growing very quickly and are expected to get even bigger.

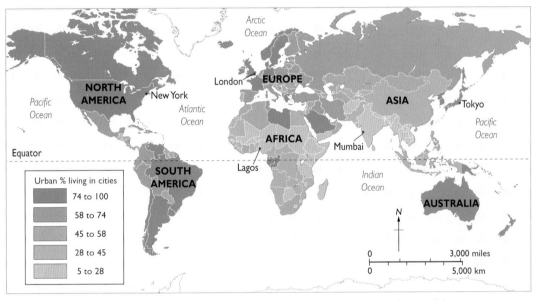

This map shows the percentage of people living in cities throughout the world.

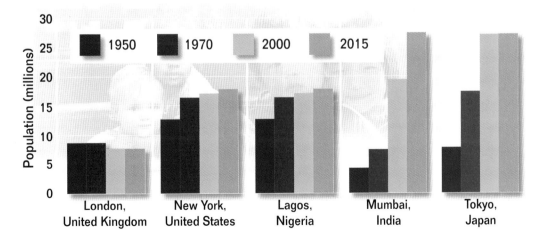

This bar chart shows how populations have changed in some cities and predicts how they might change in the future.

31

{City Strains}

There are lots of good things about living in a city. Many people who move to cities have a better chance of finding work and getting medical care and education than they did in the small towns they left behind. However, life does not always turn out as they might have hoped.

Rich and poor

Many poor people come to cities searching for a better life. Yet many find that when they arrive, there are not enough jobs for them. Or, they have to take a job with a very low rate of pay. With no money, it can be very difficult to find a place to stay in a busy, crowded city. Some people become squatters and live in empty buildings or apartments. Others construct shelters from wood or cardboard along quiet areas of railroad track or riverbanks. Many other people live on the streets. They sleep in doorways or under bridges.

There are many reasons why people in cities become homeless, but for many the problem is poverty.

Slums

When cities grow quickly, builders cannot keep up with the demands for new houses. Many of the people who need homes most are too poor to pay for them. So, many poor people live in dangerous, overcrowded, and unplanned settlements. Slums like this lack **sanitation**, such as clean water and proper washing and toilet facilities. There is a risk of people catching diseases that can spread fast through crowded areas such as slums.

At present, over 900 million people live in slums. That is almost one in three people in the world's cities. In 30 years, that number is likely to double to two billion.

Megacities!

In 2002 there were seventeen megacities across the world. Megacities are cities with over ten million inhabitants. In most of these cities, there is a huge difference between the **standard of living** of rich and poor people. By 2015 people think that over twenty cities will be this big.

Buenos Aires, Argentina, is one of the largest cities in the world. Some of its people live in comfortable, modern buildings in the center of the city. Many poor people live in "shantytowns" like this along its edge.

{Settlement and Transportation}

When you look at a map or aerial (from the sky) photograph of a settlement, one of the things you notice is the transportation network. Railroad lines, roads, lanes, canals, and cycle paths criss-cross villages, towns, and cities like spiders' webs.

Getting around

Transportation is an essential part of all settlements. In **less-developed countries**, there are fewer cars. The main ways people travel around or between villages in **rural** areas are by bike or on foot. In bigger cities and in **more-developed countries**, people use passenger transportation, such as cars, buses, and trains, to get to school, work, or to visit friends. Transportation **infrastructure** means the systems of roads, bridges, and tunnels that vehicles use. These systems affect the layout and appearance of settlements across the world.

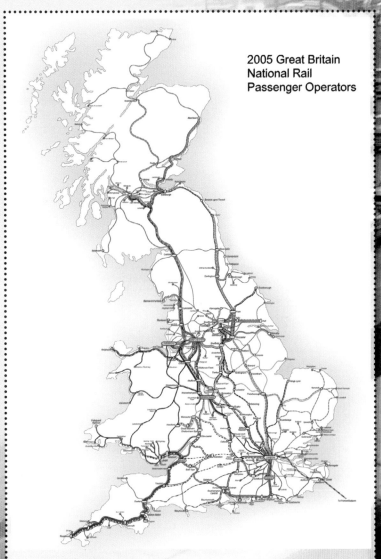

2005 Great Britain National Rail Passenger Operators

Roads and railroad lines are often called the arteries of a country like Great Britain. People compare them to the blood vessels in a human body because they are vital to the life of a city, just as arteries are essential for human life.

Long distance

Transportation between settlements is just as important as trips made within towns and cities every day. In addition to the trips for business or pleasure that people take between settlements in their own or different countries, freight transportation also travels long distances. Freight transportation means the trains and trucks that bring goods to settlements. They deliver many things, including mail and newspapers, food to fill supermarket shelves, and fuel for gas stations. These goods may have traveled from across the world by ship or by plane, so **ports** and airports outside settlements are also vitally important to them.

Underground and overground

As settlements get busier and streets get more crowded, people find new ways of transporting passengers. Many cities have underground systems, where trains travel through long, underground tunnels between places. Some cities have overhead railroads, which travel on raised lines above the streets.

Airports like this one in Paris, France, are usually built near the largest settlements in a country, but railroads and highways lead out from them in all directions.

{Pollution and Congestion}

As more and more people move into cities, the number of cars and other vehicles increases. The increased amount of traffic causes **congestion** and **pollution**.

Too many cars

Traffic congestion is when there are too many cars in an area. Today, cars take up one-third of the available space in many cities. This leads to traffic jams, when lines of cars are forced to slow down or stop. Traffic congestion causes serious pollution because these cars sit with their engines running, pumping exhaust fumes into the air.

Congestion solutions

City planners are trying to solve congestion problems by building ring roads, or bypasses. These are roads that circle around a city to keep traffic out of busy town centers. Many cities also have "Park and Ride" systems, in which people park their cars outside a city and then take buses to the center. Keeping cars out of city centers also leaves more space for parks and people.

In some cities, cyclists have to wear masks to filter out the exhaust fumes from cars and other vehicles.

Pollution

Air pollution from vehicle exhaust pipes causes serious breathing problems among some city dwellers. In many cities, there are high rates of asthma, especially among children. Asthma is a condition that makes it hard for people to breathe normally. Air pollution can also cause other serious problems, such as heart disease and **cancers**, that can be fatal.

Take the bus!

Private cars are major contributors to city air pollution. This chart shows the percentage of people in four different parts of the world who use trains or buses to get to and around cities. Although the chart compares countries and cities that are very different sizes, it shows how the numbers of people using public transportation vary in different places.

In many countries, governments are working on ways to encourage more people to leave their cars at home. If more people around the world use public transportation, the levels of pollution and congestion can be drastically reduced. Walking or cycling to a train station or bus stop would also make people fitter and healthier.

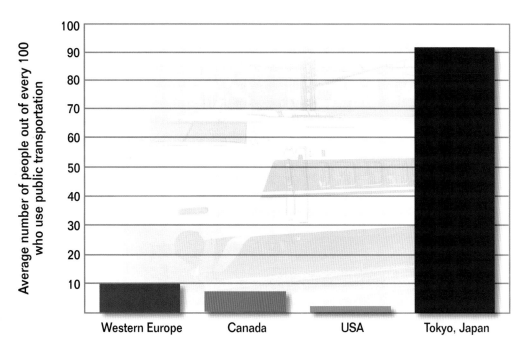

This bar chart shows the number of people out of every 100 who use public transportation in different places.

{Settlements and Resources}

Settlements grow as the **population** increases. And as settlements grow, there are more demands on the world's **natural resources**, such as water, trees, and land. In some places, this has created serious problems.

Supply and demand

Some cities face a shortage of water because households, farms, and factories have used so much. In many places, large areas of forest have been cut down to provide wood for cooking, timber for building, or clear land for farming. Where farmers have had to plow and spray the land agressively to produce extra food, the soil has dried out and turned to dust. Smoke and fumes from factories, which supply the goods that people want, **pollute** the air.

FACT!

Cities account for 80 percent of world use of fossil fuels.

*The large numbers of people in a big city like Cairo, Egypt, create a massive amount of waste. Poor people create less waste than wealthy people do because they have little money to buy things they don't really need. Here, poor families make a living by **recycling** other people's waste.*

Energy

Cities, directly and indirectly, are responsible for the bulk of the planet's energy consumption. Everything we consume or use, including our homes, cars, clothes, and the food we eat, requires energy. It takes energy to produce and package them, to distribute them to stores or front doors, to operate them, and then to get rid of them. Most of the energy that powers our settlements and transportation comes from **fossil fuels**. Oil, coal, and gas are fossil fuels. They formed from the remains of plants that lived millions of years ago. Fossil fuels are **non-renewable resources**. They take millions of years to form, so they cannot be replaced and will run out one day.

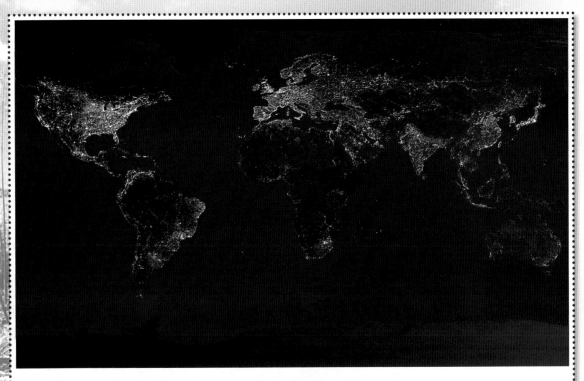

This is a view of Earth from space at night. Looking at all the lit-up areas is a great way of seeing where the most densely populated areas of the planet are. It also gives you an idea of how much energy settlements across the world are using to light their homes and streets.

{Investigating City Solutions}

The challenges facing settlements today are not all about numbers of people. They have more to do with the inequality of the ways we use and share the planet's **natural resources**. There is enough space in the world for millions more people, and there should be enough natural resources to provide food, homes, and clothes for us all. We just have to find ways to use resources in a fair and **sustainable** way.

Sustainable cities

Many city planners are investigating ways to build new kinds of settlements. If a town has more cycle lanes and safe walking paths, people can travel without using cars. Some new houses are built to use **solar power**. Solar power is electricity made using energy from the Sun. It is a **renewable resource** and produces no **pollution**. Sustainable settlements also have good **recycling** plans. These collect paper, cans, plastic, and glass and greatly reduce the amount of waste that cities produce.

Time for trees

Planting more trees and ensuring there is room for parks and green spaces is important in cities. Tree leaves give out oxygen and take in carbon dioxide, the gas in the air that causes pollution, to make their food. As they do so, they also remove the tiny bits of soot dumped in the air by car exhausts. So, trees not only make a city look nicer, they also clean the air and help people breathe more easily.

Sustainable settlements

The picture below shows some of the 500 new houses in Tango, a colorful housing complex in the Swedish city of Malmö. This city is an example of the way sustainable cities of the future could be. Tango was built on abandoned, polluted land that was once used by industries but was then cleaned up and reclaimed.

The buildings here are linked to a water system that recycles its water into a marsh, where reed plants help filter and clean used water. The electricity is made from renewable sources, such as solar power and wind energy. The windows are large, letting in as much light as possible and thus reducing the amount of electricity used. They also have three layers of glass to reduce the amount of heating required. All toilets, sinks, and electrical devices are energy efficient, and there is a pipe system that collects waste for recycling. Traffic is carefully controlled to make it easy for walkers and cyclists to get around, and there are bus stops every 330 yards (300 meters) to encourage people to use public transportation. Can you imagine living in a city like this one day?

{The Future}

In the future, more and more people will move to and settle in big cities. People who plan cities and the governments that run them will have to think carefully about ways to ensure that these **urban** settlements are safe, healthy, and happy places to live.

In the past, cities have often grown too fast and people have been left in poor, inadequate housing. This has taught us that cities need to ensure that everyone has a good drinking water supply and adequate **sanitation**.

In the future, there will be more pressure on **resources** as cities grow in the **less-developed countries**. People there may begin to buy as many new things and use up as much energy and fuel as people in the **more-developed countries** do today. This would put a huge strain on nature and the world's **natural resources**. The challenge will be for cities to improve **recycling** systems. It's also important that everyone limit the demands they make on resources by using less and buying less.

Challenges

The other challenge for cities of the future is transportation. Many cities have grown by simply spreading out from a central point. This has meant that people have to travel a long way from the **suburbs** to work or to shop. Some cities in the more-developed world already have several well-equipped centers that can supply the needs of the people nearby without requiring them to travel far. This type of development will need to become more common in big cities around the world.

*One day, cities may use more electric buses like this one. It does not use gasoline or diesel, so it causes little **pollution**.*

What we can do

More and more people today care about the **environment**, and there are lots of things that we can all do to improve life in our settlement and save natural resources. These things may sound like small changes, but if everyone did them, it would make a big difference.

- Don't drop litter. It looks bad and it can harm animals if they eat old food or get trapped in old cans. Rotting waste can also spread disease.

- You can **compost**. Reduce food waste and get a compost bin that turns old food into new compost to help your garden grow.

- Turn off lights and machines when you leave a room and take showers instead of baths. Finding ways to save energy and water cuts down on the natural resources used.

- Cycle or walk to school and to visit friends, if you can. It's better for you and the environment.

- Organize your household waste into recycling bins and reduce waste wherever you can.

These children are turning an ugly patch of wasteland into a colorful garden that will attract birds and butterflies—as well as people.

{Further Resources}

Books

Aykroyd, Clarissa. *Refugees*. Philadelphia: Mason Crest, 2004.

Dalton, Dave. *Economic Migrants*. Chicago: Heinemann Library, 2006.

Dalton, Dave. *Refugees and Asylum Seekers*. Chicago: Heinemann Library, 2006.

Senker, Cath. *Why Are People Refugees?* Chicago: Raintree, 2005.

Smith, Trevor. *Migrants and Refugees*. North Mankato, Minn.: Smart Apple Media, 2004.

Aid organizations

If you feel you would like to help refugees or other people in need, try visiting the website of one of the following aid organizations:

The Red Cross, at http://www.redcross.org.

Save the Children, at http://www.savethechildren.org.

UNICEF, at http://www.unicef.org.

Flug Flight		nach to	über via	planm. scheduled	verspätet delayed	Schalter Counter
LG	302	LUXEMBURG		930		113-33
AZ	419	TURIN		935		339-34
LH	1122	NEAPEL		935		113-33
LH	1906	MADRID		935		113-33
LH	1022	STUTTGART HBF.		935		–
AF	1701	LYON		940		683-64
AY	822	HELSINKI		940		113-3
AA	071	SFRANCISCO-DALLAS		945		731-7
AF	743	PARIS		945		683-6
LH	1116	VENEDIG		945		113-3
DL	023	DALLAS		950		478-4
GA	892	AMSTERDAM		950		721-7

{ Glossary }

archaeologist someone who studies human history by finding and looking at objects from the distant past

cancer disease in which abnormal cells grow and spread. Cancer can be fatal.

civil war war between groups of people in the same country

climate general conditions of weather in an area

compost to convert rotted garden and food waste into a mixture used for fertilizing

congestion when there is too much traffic and the roads are overcrowded

emigrate to leave one country to go to another. Someone who emigrates is called an emigrant.

environment our surroundings: the air, land, and sea in which we live

famine when there is not enough food for a large number of people

fertile describes soil that plants grow well in

fossil fuel fuel such as oil, coal, and gas. These formed from the remains of plants and animals that lived millions of years ago. They cannot be replaced.

function main activity or purpose of a settlement—for example, a mining town or a fishing village

immigrant someone who moves or migrates to a new country from another

import buy food or goods from other countries

industry trade or business. Mining and tourism are both kinds of industry.

infrastructure basic system of roads, bridges, and tunnels that form the transportation network of a place

less-developed countries Africa, most of Asia, Latin America and the Caribbean, and Oceania (except for Australia and New Zealand)

metropolis large, busy city

migrant workers people who travel to a different country for long periods of time for work

migrate move from one place to live in another. **Migration** is the process of migrating.

more-developed countries wealthier, more industrialized countries of the world, including the United States, Canada, Europe, Australia, New Zealand, and Japan

natural disaster disaster due to natural causes, such as an earthquake

natural resource thing from the natural world, such as water, that we use and need

nomadic someone who does not live in one spot, but roams from place to place

non-renewable resource material we use that will run out one day

pollution something that poisons or damages (**pollutes**) air, water, or land

population number of people

population density number of people living in an area of land—for example, people per square mile

port place where goods can be brought into a country or sent out to other countries by ship

recycle change waste into something that can be used again

refugee someone who has been forced to flee his or her home to escape danger and is afraid to return there

renewable resource resource that regenerates itself, so it never runs out

resource material or other thing that people need and use

rural to do with the country

sanitation system of disposing of waste from people's bathrooms

services systems that supply people's needs, such as hospitals and hotels

site where something is

solar power means of making electricity by trapping and converting energy from the Sun

standard of living level and comfort of living conditions for people in a particular place

suburb large area of houses at the edge of a city

sustainable something that keeps going and does not run out

terrain shape, height, and type of land in an area

tsunami giant sea wave, often caused by an underwater earthquake

urban to do with towns and cities

vaccination injection of a dead or weakened sample of an infection that stops people from getting the disease later

{Index}